SUMMER FRIENDS

by Jane Porter Meier

Cover Illustration: Paul Micich
Inside Illustration: Larassa Kabel

I would like to dedicate this book to my grandmother, Emma Jane Hughey. Her love and encouragement has been with me every day of my life.

About the Author

Jane Porter Meier has taught children from preschool through third grade for 25 years. She is now retired from teaching but still substitute teaches in many different schools. And at one time, she was a newspaper reporter.

Mrs. Meier received a bachelor of arts degree at the University of Nebraska and a master's degree in reading at Pepperdine University.

Mrs. Meier lives in California, close to Disneyland. She has three sons, four grandchildren, and two great-grandchildren.

Text © 2000 by Perfection Learning® Corporation.

All rights reserved. No part of this book may be used or reproduced in any manner whatsoever without written permission from the publisher.

Printed in the United States of America. For information, contact

Perfection Learning® Corporation

Phone: 1-800-831-4190

Fax: 1-712-644-2392

1000 North Second Avenue, P.O. Box 500

Logan, Iowa 51546-0500.

Paperback ISBN 0-7891-2927-2

Cover Craft® ISBN 0-7807-8964-4

Printed in the U.S.A.

6 7 8 9 10 PP 09 08 07 06 05

Contents

1
Joey

Cassiopeia Foster sat on the porch swing at Aunt Diane's house. Tears trickled down her suntanned cheeks. She brushed the tears away with the back of her hand.

What am I going to do for a whole summer? Cassie thought miserably. There's nothing to do in dumb old Nebraska City!

Cassie sunk back against bright yellow cushions. She closed her eyes. She could see her friends back in sunny southern California.

I'll bet they're going to the beach every day, she thought. And having so much fun!

Cassie blew her nose loudly. She sighed and picked up *Growin' Pains,* a book she had been reading. But the words on the page just jumbled together. They didn't make sense.

Cassie couldn't concentrate. She slammed the book shut. Then she tossed it on the table.

I just don't understand, she said to herself. Why don't Mom and Dad love each other anymore? How can people just stop loving each other?

I love them both so much, Cassie thought. I miss them. *And* I miss California.

Cassie sighed. Here she was—stuck with Aunt Diane. Because of the divorce and all. Her mom had thought it would be better for Cassie. But Cassie wasn't so sure.

Scritch . . . scratch . . . squeak. Aunt Diane's porch swing creaked as Cassie swung back and forth.

Cassie stared out the huge screened porch windows. Rows and rows of apple trees covered the land as far as she could see. She could see Henry Weatherhog, the hired helper, working among the trees.

Cassie remembered visiting Nebraska City when the trees were in full bloom. It looked like popcorn popping everywhere. But this time she'd come too late to see the beautiful blossoms.

It had been so much fun then, Cassie thought. When Grandpa had been alive. He'd always had a pony for her to ride. What fun it had been on fat little Dixie's back! They would canter through Arbor Lodge Park. Or sometimes they would gallop through the orchards.

Cassie had ridden Dixie across the pasture. They'd stopped beside the rippling stream for a picnic. Cassie could still remember the peanut butter sandwiches, cold milk from a thermos, and juicy apples from Grandpa's orchard.

Cassie always saved an apple for Dixie. Grandpa had shown her how to hold it with her hand out flat. That way, Dixie could nibble the apple without biting Cassie's hand.

Cassie closed her eyes. She could see Grandpa's smiling face. His cheeks were always pink. Probably from working outside in his orchards for so many years. His green eyes would twinkle when he played a trick on Cassie. Or when he called her his little strawberry—because of her hair. How he had loved to tease her!

Grandpa had never seemed old to Cassie. She remembered when Aunt Diane had phoned from Nebraska with the news. Grandpa had died.

Cassie and her mother were shocked and terribly sad. Cassie had cried. It wasn't fair that people you loved so much had to die.

Cassie stood up from the porch swing. She walked outside and leaned on the white picket fence in front of Aunt Diane's house.

Arbor Lodge Park was across the street. Cassie stared at the old, leafy trees. It's a pretty park, she thought. And I like living across the street from it.

But thinking about the park didn't cheer her.

After a while, Cassie heard giggling and loud voices. A group of children was walking down Park Avenue. They were carrying brown lunch sacks and lunch boxes. They were having so much fun.

Cassie looked longingly at the children. But none of them glanced her way.

So Cassie sat down on the porch steps. She buried her face in her hands. She had a hollow feeling in her stomach.

When Cassie looked up, she saw a boy in a wheelchair. He was moving toward the park.

Just as the boy went through the park gate, one of his wheels got caught in a rut. His wheelchair tilted to one side. Cassie could see that he couldn't get his wheelchair out of the rut.

Cassie knew that people in wheelchairs didn't always want help. But after watching him struggle more, she jumped up and raced across the street.

Cassie stood in front of him so he would see her. "Can I help?" she asked.

"I think I'm going to need it," the boy said.

Cassie walked behind the boy. Grabbing hold of the wheelchair, she pushed with all her strength. Finally, the wheelchair bumped up out of the rut. Cassie walked around in front of the boy again.

"Hey, thanks," said the boy.

Cassie looked into the most beautiful blue eyes she had ever seen.

"No problem," Cassie said.

"I don't remember seeing you around here," the boy said.

Cassie twisted a lock of her strawberry blond hair. "I'm spending the summer with my Aunt Diane." Cassie pointed to her Aunt Diane's house.

"My name's Joey Ryan," said the boy. "I live with my Granny Lee. Our house is just down the dirt road. The one behind your aunt's house."

"We're kind of neighbors then," said Cassie. "I'm Cassiopeia Foster. But everyone calls me Cassie."

"Nice to meet you," said Joey. He leaned forward to push the wheels of his chair. "Well, see you around." And he rolled on into the park.

Cassie walked back across the street. She sat down on the porch steps. She wondered why Joey was in a wheelchair. Whatever the reason, she felt bad for him. But she was glad that he lived near Aunt Diane.

Cassie thought maybe she'd found a friend. And she couldn't think of anything she needed more.

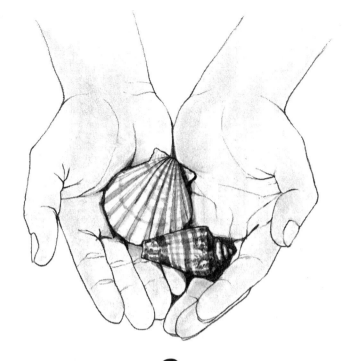

2
The Wheels Are Turning

Cassie awoke early the next morning. Princess, Aunt Diane's dog, was barking outside her bedroom window.

Probably barking at the neighbor's cat, Cassie thought sleepily.

Cassie rolled out of bed and padded to the window. She pulled back the white lace curtains. Sure enough, Princess was racing back and forth, barking loudly. And there was the black-and-white cat, Misty.

Misty sat on top of the toolshed, cleaning herself. Her furry black tail swished back and forth. She stopped licking her paws and stared down at Princess.

"Be still, Princess," whispered Cassie. "You'll wake up Aunt Diane and the neighbors."

Princess stopped barking for a second and looked up at Cassie. But then she continued yapping at the cat.

Cassie was wide-awake now. She decided that she might as well get up. So she put on her shorts and T-shirt. As she brushed her hair, she thought about Joey.

I'm going to go and see Joey today, Cassie decided. I need a friend here.

It was going to be a hot day. So Cassie pulled her hair back in a ponytail.

Then she had an idea. She dug through her dresser drawer and found two very special seashells. She'd found them on the beach in California. She put them in the pocket of her shorts. Then she hurried into the kitchen.

Cassie gulped down a glass of orange juice. Then she grabbed two cinnamon rolls from a paper bag and dashed out the door.

Cassie walked down the bumpy dirt road behind the house. She munched on one of the cinnamon rolls. As she rounded a bend in the road, she saw a small white house. It was surrounded with roses.

Cassie had never seen roses of so many different

colors. Red, pink, white, lavender, and yellow. And the most beautiful of all to Cassie—apricot-colored roses.

This must be where Joey lives, Cassie thought.

Suddenly, Cassie felt nervous about going up to the door. But just then, it opened. A small, gray-haired woman came out and saw Cassie standing there.

"Why, hello," the lady said with a smile.

Cassie noticed that the old lady had only one tooth in her mouth. It was in the middle of her lower gum. It had made a neat little groove in her pink upper gum.

But what Cassie noticed the most were the old lady's eyes. They were soft, brown, and kind.

"Is this where Joey lives?" Cassie asked.

"It sure is, honey," answered the old lady. "He's a lazy boy this morning. He's not up yet."

"Oh," said Cassie. "I'll come back later then."

"Oh, no, child," said Granny Lee. "You come on in. I'm Joey's Granny Lee. Now you just sit right here while I wake up that lazybones." She pointed to a rocking chair.

There was not much furniture inside the little house. But everything was neat and clean. A faded blue sofa, a worn armchair, a table, and a spinet piano filled the small living room. A picture of a beautiful little girl sat on top of the piano. Beside the picture was a bouquet of pink and lavender roses.

Before long, a door opened. Joey rolled his

wheelchair into the living room. He smiled when he saw Cassie.

"Hi," Joey said.

Cassie returned the smile. "Hi," she said. She reached into her pocket for the seashells. "Here, I brought you these. They're from the beach in California where I live. I have lots of them."

Joey's blue eyes shone with pleasure. "Hey, thanks a lot," he said, touching the pink shells. "It must be really cool to go to the beach whenever you want."

"It's pretty nice, all right," Cassie said. "I miss it."

Then there was an awkward silence. Cassie twisted a lock of her hair. Joey looked at the shells. He kept turning them over in his hands.

"I guess you met Granny Lee," Joey finally said.

Cassie nodded her head. "She's nice."

"Want to go outside?" asked Joey. "I'll show you Granny's well."

"Okay," said Cassie as she followed Joey out the back door.

Cassie stood on tiptoe and peered down into the well. Little sparkles danced on the water far below.

"It sure is a long way down there!" Cassie remarked.

"Yeah," said Joey. "The water's real cold. Want some?"

"Sure," said Cassie.

Joey reached up and grabbed a rope. One part of the rope was tied to a pole. The rope lay over a wheel hanging from the cover above the well. The other end of the rope went down into the well. Joey untied the rope from the pole.

Cassie peered over the edge of the well to watch. Joey pulled and pulled on the rope. Finally, up came an old oak bucket with water dripping from its sides.

Joey filled a dipper with water from the bucket. "Here," he said. "Taste it."

Cassie took a long drink. "It's ice-cold!" she said. "I've never seen a well before."

Joey rolled over to a wooden bench. It had been built to go around a huge oak tree trunk.

"It's hot already," said Joey. "Let's sit in the shade."

Cassie sat down by Joey. She wanted to ask him why he was in a wheelchair. But she wasn't sure if she should. So they sat in silence for a while. Then they both started to talk at the same time. And that made them both laugh.

"I guess you're wondering why I'm in a wheelchair," said Joey.

Cassie nodded.

Joey looked across the yard at a beautiful lilac bush. It was loaded with purple blossoms.

"Well," Joey began. "Two years ago, my parents and I were in a car accident. It happened at the curve of the highway. Not far from your aunt's house. My mom and dad were killed instantly. And I was left like this—unable to walk."

Cassie didn't know what to say. She hadn't expected to hear anything this horrible. She could tell that Joey was sad. But he was trying hard not to show it. Her heart ached for him.

"I'm really sorry, Joey," she said, feeling how empty her words were.

"Granny Lee took me in," Joey continued. "She's not my real grandmother. But I feel like she is. She took care of my mom when my mom was a little girl. Like, you know—Granny was her nanny."

Cassie nodded her head. She struggled to keep the tears that stung her eyes from spilling over.

Joey rolled over to the driveway that ran alongside Granny Lee's house. "Hey, Cassie," Joey said. His happy smile was back again. "Want to see me do a wheelie in my chair?"

"Sure," said Cassie.

Joey whirled his wheelchair around. He picked up speed as he went down the driveway. Then he spun around on one wheel.

"Cool!" said Cassie, admiring Joey's courage.

Joey rolled back to the bench. "Are you ever going to be able to walk again?" Cassie asked.

"Well," said Joey. "If I had enough money, I could go to this hospital in Omaha. There's a doctor there that can sometimes fix guys like me. I guess she fits braces on people's legs and stuff like that."

The wheels were turning in Cassie's head. "How much does that cost?" she asked.

"I don't know, but it's an awful lot," Joey said.

Cassie leaned back on the bench in the cool shade of the beautiful old tree. She twisted a lock of strawberry blond hair.

"You know what?" Cassie said at last.

"What?" replied Joey.

"I'll bet we could earn some money this summer. And maybe you could get to Omaha to that doctor."

Joey looked puzzled. "How?" he asked.

"Just let me think about it," Cassie said as she ran toward the front yard. "See you later."

3
A Great Idea

Later, as Aunt Diane made lunch, Cassie talked about the morning. Cassie helped herself to a raw carrot. "Oh, Aunt Diane, I feel so bad for Joey," she said as she crunched the carrot. "He lost his parents in an accident. And he can't walk. But there's a doctor in Omaha who might be able to help him walk again."

Aunt Diane dried her hands on a towel. Then she walked over to Cassie. She took Cassie's face in both of her hands.

"Your mother said you'd be into something after a few days," Aunt Diane smiled. "And I guess this is it."

"Oh, Aunt Diane!" Cassie said. "I don't think his granny has much money. I sure wish I could help him."

Aunt Diane sat down beside Cassie. They continued to talk about Joey through lunch.

After lunch, Cassie ran down the dirt road to Joey's house. Princess bounded along, wagging her fluffy tail.

Joey was watering Granny Lee's roses when Cassie arrived.

Princess bounded up to Joey and licked his hand. Then she plunked two big paws on Joey's legs and gave his cheek a quick, loving lick.

Cassie's cheeks were pink from running.

"Well, have you thought of anything yet?" Cassie panted.

Joey shook his head. "Not yet," he said.

"I haven't either," said Cassie. "But I will."

Joey lifted the hose and aimed the spray at Cassie.

"Hey, cut that out!" said Cassie, giggling.

Princess snapped at the water. She tried to get a drink but got her nose wet instead.

After Joey had watered the roses, he and Cassie took Princess for a walk in the park. Cassie told Joey all about her hometown. She told him about her parents' divorce. Finally, it was time for Cassie to go home.

Cassie skipped along with Princess trotting by her side. She thought of her mom and dad. She missed them. And even though she was upset about the divorce, she was glad that she had a mom and dad. She wished Joey could feel that way.

I'm going to help him see that doctor so he can walk again, Cassie vowed.

✳ ✳ ✳ ✳ ✳

At 8:00 Saturday morning, Joey rolled up the walk at Aunt Diane's house. Drops of sweat trickled down his forehead. He waved when he saw Cassie.

"Man!" Joey said. "It's hot today!" He pulled a handkerchief from his pocket and mopped at his face.

Cassie and Aunt Diane turned Joey's wheelchair around. Together, they backed him up the steps and into the kitchen.

The scent of cookies baking welcomed Cassie and Joey. Sugar-cookie dough sat in a big yellow mixing bowl. It was ready to go onto a greased cookie sheet.

"Here, Joey," said Cassie. "You can drop the cookie dough onto the cookie sheet."

"Okay," said Joey. Aunt Diane was helping him wash his hands at the sink.

As they ate warm cookies, Joey told Cassie a little more about the town. There was a movie theater nearby, so they planned to see a movie while Cassie was visiting.

"Well, have you thought of anything yet?" Joey asked.

"Not yet," said Cassie. "But I can always think better when I'm eating." And she grabbed another cookie.

"You know this neighborhood better than I do," said Cassie. "Where could we get hired to do some odd jobs?"

"Well," said Joey, brushing cookie crumbs from his lap. "Mr. and Mrs. Wolf live over at Wildwood. It's a big place. Maybe they'd hire us. Some things I can't do. But there's a lot I *can* do."

"What is Wildwood anyway?" Cassie wondered.

"Granny Lee told me that a man with a lot of money once lived there," Joey explained. "His name was Mr. Whitfield. When he died, he gave the place to Nebraska City. People can go through the old house on tours if they want to."

"Let's go right now," said Cassie. "Is Wildwood very far from here?"

"Nothing's very far from anywhere in this little place," said Joey.

So after rinsing their dirty dishes, Cassie and Joey set off for Wildwood. Cassie wanted to push Joey's wheelchair, but he wouldn't let her.

"Rolling myself helps me keep my arms and upper

body strong," Joey said. "Then, if I ever get my legs to work again . . ." His voice trailed off.

"You know," said Cassie. "People here in Nebraska City have the weirdest names. Wolf and Weatherhog. Can you think of any more weird names?"

"Sure," said Joey. "One of the teachers at my school is named Ima. She has a sister named Ura. And their last name is Hogg."

Cassie cracked up. So as they walked, they thought up more funny names.

"How about a man named Pete?" said Joey. "Pete Moss!"

"Or a lady named Rose?" said Cassie, thinking of Granny Lee's roses. "Rose Garden! Or Rose Thorn! Or Rose Bush!"

"How about Jess?" laughed Joey. "Jess Taminute!"

Cassie walked along beside Joey as they traveled toward Wildwood. They made up funny names the whole way there.

4
Wildwood

Cassie and Joey were thirsty when they arrived at Wildwood. They both took long gulps of cool water from a water fountain. Then Cassie pushed Joey over to a tree. She sank down on the thick grass in the shade of a big, leafy maple tree. She leaned against its gnarled trunk.

"I should warn you," said Joey. "Mr. Wolf *looks* an awful lot like a wolf."

"Is his first name Gray?" laughed Cassie. "Or We're? Or Hungry?"

Joey laughed too.

"It's sure pretty here," said Cassie, looking around. "The lawn looks like green velvet."

Just then, a man in bib overalls walked around the red barn. He was wearing a broad-brimmed yellow straw hat.

"Hi, Mr. Wolf," called Joey. He turned his wheelchair around to face Mr. Wolf.

Mr. Wolf strolled to where the children were sitting under the tree. He squinted his beady eyes at Joey.

"Do I know you?" Mr. Wolf asked.

"I'm Joey Ryan, Mr. Wolf," Joey replied. "I live with Mrs. Lee over by Mr. Potter's apple orchard." Joey pointed in the direction of Granny Lee's house. "And this is my friend, Cassie Foster. She's from California."

Cassie smiled. "Hi, Mr. Wolf," she said. He really *does* look like a wolf, she thought.

"Well, what are you two doing here?" asked Mr. Wolf.

Joey was twisting a button on his shirt. He didn't say anything. So Cassie spoke up.

"We wondered if you might have some work we could do around here," she said. "We need to earn some money." Cassie hesitated. "We can do lots of things."

Mr. Wolf took off his straw hat and scratched his head. He pulled a wrinkled red handkerchief from his overall pocket and mopped his brow with it.

He looks even more like a wolf without his hat on, Cassie noticed. But she kept her eyes on Mr. Wolf. She was afraid she'd giggle if she looked at Joey.

"Well, I'll go up to the house and talk to Mrs. Wolf," said Mr. Wolf. "We'll see what we can come up with." And then he walked around to the back of Wildwood House.

Cassie put her hand to her mouth. She didn't want Mr. Wolf to hear her laughing.

"Why did you tell me that Mr. Wolf looks like a wolf?" she said between fits of laughter. "It was hard to keep from laughing."

"Well, doesn't he?" laughed Joey. He turned his head away from the house so no one would see him laugh.

"Yes, he really does," said Cassie. "But if you hadn't said anything, maybe I wouldn't have thought about it. But knowing me, I probably would have. I get into loads of trouble at school when something strikes me funny. Sometimes I just can't stop laughing."

"I know what you mean," said Joey. "You know, when you laugh or smile, you've got great big dimples."

Cassie touched her cheek. "I don't like them much," she said. "But I guess they're here to stay."

Before long, both Mr. and Mrs. Wolf came out of the house. She was a short, plump little lady with a round face and chubby cheeks. Her frizzy red hair stuck out on the sides and it was flat on top.

Cassie thought Mr. and Mrs. Wolf didn't go together at all. Mrs. Wolf reminded Cassie of one of her friend's dogs—a plump little Pekingese named Sugar.

"This is my wife," said Mr. Wolf. "And this is Cassie and Joey."

"Hi," Cassie and Joey said.

Mrs. Wolf looked at Cassie and Joey for a long time. She cocked her head to one side, just like Sugar. Mrs. Wolf seemed to be studying them.

"So you kids want to earn some money this summer?" Mrs. Wolf said at last.

Cassie and Joey nodded their heads.

"Yes, ma'am. We do," said Cassie.

"Well, Mr. Wolf and I have an awful lot of work to do around this place," she said. She looked sharply at Joey. "Son, do you think you can water our roses? And wash off the walks and the driveway every day?"

"Yes, ma'am. I sure can," said Joey.

"And don't forget the gazebo, Bess," chimed in Mr. Wolf.

"That's right," said Mrs. Wolf. "That gazebo and the benches inside it need to be hosed off daily too."

Mrs. Wolf stared at Cassie. "And you, missy," she

said. "You can help me in the house with dusting and dishes and the like."

"That's fine," Cassie said. She sure doesn't act like Sugar, though, Cassie thought. She's too sour.

"Now for your pay," said Mr. Wolf. "How does four dollars an hour for the two of you together sound? And we'd like you to work about two hours a day, Monday through Friday." His grin showed yellow, crooked teeth.

Cassie and Joey looked at each other. "Fine," they said together.

"You can start Monday then," said Mrs. Wolf. "That way, you can still have some fun each day." She smiled warmly at the two children. "I always say that kids should have lots of fun while they're kids."

"Yes, ma'am," said Cassie. "And we sure do thank you both a lot."

"Well, then. Good-bye for now," said Mr. Wolf. "We'll expect you Monday, about 9:00." Then he and his wife headed for their house.

"See you then," called Joey.

"I'm going to push you home whether you want me to or not," said Cassie. She took hold of the handles of Joey's wheelchair. "Just think, Joey. Between us, we'll earn eight dollars a day."

"Yeah," said Joey. "And five times eight is forty. Wow! We'll make forty dollars a week! And we'll still have time to have some fun."

When Cassie and Joey got to the end of the driveway, Cassie turned the wheelchair to the right. As she did, she glanced back at Wildwood.

"Joey, look," Cassie said. "See that tall man in the black suit? He's creeping around toward the back of the gazebo. He looks weird. Kind of sneaky. Like he doesn't want anyone to see him or something."

Joey looked back just as the man disappeared behind the gazebo.

"Hmm," Joey said. "I didn't get a real good look at him. But he kind of looks like Granny Lee's brother, Ed." He looked concerned. "I sure hope it's not."

"Why do you say that?" Cassie asked.

"On account of Granny Lee says her brother Ed's no good," Joey answered. "And she doesn't want him at her house. He just sponges off of her. And he never pays for anything. Seems like he's nothing but trouble."

"Oh," said Cassie. "Well, maybe it's just someone who looks like Granny Lee's brother. Let's hope so!"

5
A Ghostly Shadow

Thunder rumbled across the black night sky. Rain beat against the window. Flashes of lightning lit Cassie's bedroom. Cassie pulled the sheet up over her head.

Thunderstorms didn't happen very often in California. And this storm scared her. Especially when she thought of the weird man she and Joey had seen earlier.

Through the sheet, Cassie could still see the brilliant flashes of lightning. She rolled over on her side, away from the window. CRASH! The deafening crack of thunder sounded like it had ripped open the sky.

Cassie peeked out from under the sheet. The lace curtains were waving eerily. They looked like ghosts floating through the air.

I should get up and close the window, Cassie thought. But she was too scared to leave the safety of her bed.

Suddenly, the door flew open. Aunt Diane hurried into the room, her flowered robe flying behind her. Her slippers shuffled against the carpet.

"Terrible storm," Aunt Diane muttered as she crossed to the window.

The window came down with a loud smack. Aunt Diane walked over to Cassie's bed. She pulled the sheet from Cassie's head.

"You all right, honey?" Aunt Diane asked.

"I guess," said Cassie. "But I'm scared, Aunt Diane. We hardly ever have storms like this in California."

"I know," said Aunt Diane. "But you do have earthquakes out there. I'd be more afraid of those."

Cassie didn't answer. Her head was covered up with the sheet again.

"Don't be afraid, Cassie," Aunt Diane said. "It'll be over soon. You're safe and snug in your bed."

Aunt Diane said good night and went back to her room.

Finally, the storm stopped. It seemed like it had lasted for hours.

Cassie was just dropping off to sleep when Princess began barking. Then Cassie heard a low growl.

Princess never barks at night, thought Cassie.

She knew that Misty was in the garage for the night. So Princess wasn't barking at her.

Still the low growl continued. Then loud barking.

Cassie slid out of bed. She tiptoed over to the window. Standing to the side, she pulled back the curtain.

Outside, it was pitch black except on the far side of the garage. There, a small lightbulb cast an eerie orange glow. Cassie could barely see Princess at the corner of the garage.

A low growl came out of the darkness. Then frantic barking again. Cassie strained to see into the black night.

Was that a tall figure standing by the dark side of the garage? She leaned closer to the window, straining her eyes to see better.

Suddenly, there was movement. The tall shape melted out of the shadows. Whoever or whatever it was seemed to fly over the back fence and disappear into the night.

What next? Cassie thought, trembling. First, the awful storm. And now, someone or something was lurking in their backyard.

Should she tell Aunt Diane? Cassie wondered. Cassie decided not to awaken her aunt. She would tell her in the morning.

Cassie reached to turn off a small lamp on the bedside table. Then she remembered the tall man she and Joey had seen at Wildwood. The shadowy figure had seemed like a tall person. Could the shadow figure in the backyard be the same person they had seen yesterday? Cassie sighed. Probably not, she decided. She was imagining things now.

Cassie tried to forget about the scary night. She thought about her mom and dad in California. She missed them a lot. And she wished that they weren't getting divorced.

But I know they both still love me, she thought. They tell me that all the time.

Cassie realized that she wasn't as lonely now as she had been before. I guess it's because I know Joey, she thought.

As she rolled over in bed, Cassie's mind drifted. She thought of the work they were going to do at Wildwood.

I really want to help Joey, she thought just before she fell asleep.

6
Work for Nothing

Cassie was up early on Monday. It was her first day of work at Wildwood. She skipped down the dirt road toward Joey's house.

The air was cool. But the rising sun promised a hot day ahead.

Cassie peeked through Granny Lee's kitchen door. Granny Lee spied Cassie and opened the door. A spicy smell floated out to meet her.

Mmm, cookies! she thought. Yum! They smelled good. Joey had told her about Granny's cookies. She made all kinds—chocolate, peanut butter, sugar, and oatmeal. And every one of them tasted great.

Today, Granny Lee was baking oatmeal spice cookies. They were filled with raisins and nuts. The cookies were still warm when Joey put a handful into a paper bag.

"Guess we'd better get going," Joey said. "We don't want to be late on our first day."

"You're right," Cassie said as she took a bite of a warm cookie.

As Cassie walked beside Joey, she told him what she'd seen last night.

"Are you sure?" asked Joey. "Maybe it was just your imagination. What with the storm and all."

Cassie shook her head.

"No, it wasn't my imagination," she said. "The storm scared me. But I saw the shape *after* the storm was over. I saw someone jump over the back fence." She twisted her hair. "It reminded me of the man we saw at Wildwood. But I suppose that's kind of silly, isn't it?"

"Probably," mumbled Joey, wiping cookie crumbs off his lips.

Cassie slowly walked beside Joey on the bumpy sidewalk, chattering all the while. Joey just nodded yes or no to her questions. He seemed unusually quiet.

"Is anything wrong?" Cassie asked him.

Joey shook his head.

"You seem awfully quiet," said Cassie. She walked around in front of the wheelchair to look at Joey.

"Well," Joey began. "I've done a lot of thinking. I don't think you should have to spend your summer trying to earn money to help me. It just doesn't seem right." Joey's blue eyes looked troubled. He ran his fingers through his curly dark hair.

"Hey, cut it out," said Cassie. "It's something I *want* to do. It'll be fun. Besides, what else have I got to do?"

"Well, okay. If you're sure," Joey said.

"I'm sure," said Cassie with a smile. "Besides, it helps take my mind off my parents' divorce. So you're helping me too."

"I guess so," said Joey.

Cassie smiled through the tears that sparkled in her eyes.

❄ ❄ ❄ ❄ ❄

"Hi, Mr. Wolf!" called Cassie when they got to Wildwood.

Mr. Wolf stood up slowly from pulling weeds in his vegetable garden.

"Going to be a hot one again today," Mr. Wolf said. "I'll get you kids started before it gets too hot." He pulled the hose over for Joey.

"Now water those roses real good, son," Mr. Wolf said. "Then when you're done, you can hose off the walks."

Mr. Wolf squinted his beady eyes at Cassie. "Now let's see," he said scratching his head. "You come with me, missy. We'll pull weeds in the backyard. Then Mrs. Wolf has some work for you to do."

After working two hours in the hot summer sun, Joey and Cassie stopped. Then they rang the front doorbell. Mrs. Wolf came to the door with a towel wrapped around her head.

"We're finished for today, ma'am," said Cassie.

Joey and Cassie waited for Mrs. Wolf to pay them. But she made no motion to get her purse or to give them their money. She just looked at them. Finally she said, "We'll pay you at the end of the week." Then she slammed the door shut.

Cassie and Joey looked at each other.

"Well," Joey said. "I guess we'll just have to wait until Friday."

"Guess so," agreed Cassie. And they started down the road toward home.

❊ ❊ ❊ ❊ ❊

On Friday, Joey and Cassie had worked ten hours. They once again rang the Wolfs' doorbell. This time, Mr. Wolf opened the door.

"Mr. Wolf," Cassie said. "Mrs. Wolf said that you would pay us today."

Mr. Wolf looked more wolflike than ever today. His bushy gray hair kept falling over his forehead.

"Well," Mr. Wolf said. "As a matter of fact, we don't have the money to pay you today."

Cassie twisted her hair. Joey looked at Cassie. They weren't sure what to say.

Mr. Wolf broke the silence. "Go along now," he said. "We'll pay you *next* Friday."

Cassie grabbed the handles of Joey's wheelchair. She turned him around and began pushing him toward the road. They didn't talk until they had gone far from Wildwood.

"What do you think?" asked Joey. "Are they ever going to pay us?"

"They'd better," said Cassie. "We'd just better get paid. We aren't working for nothing."

7
Uncle Ed

Cassie was puzzled and disappointed. She was angry too. After all, she and Joey had worked hard at Wildwood. And in the hot summer sun! They'd done the best job they could.

I wonder, thought Cassie, if we've worked for nothing. She sighed. She wanted so much for Joey to see the doctor in Omaha.

When Cassie and Joey returned to Granny Lee's, they heard a man's voice in the kitchen. Joey rolled to the kitchen window. Then he stretched up to peer inside.

"It's Uncle Ed," Joey said. "Granny Lee's brother. The one I told you about."

Granny Lee and Uncle Ed sat at the kitchen table drinking tea. A plate filled with oatmeal cookies was between them.

"Hi, Uncle Ed," said Joey in a flat voice.

"Well, hello there, son," said Uncle Ed.

"This is Cassie Foster," said Joey. "She's visiting her Aunt Diane this summer. She lives in that green house across from Arbor Lodge Park."

"Yes, I know the place," said Uncle Ed. He nodded at Cassie while dunking a cookie into his cup of tea.

"Hi," Cassie said.

Cassie thought that Granny Lee looked troubled. She wasn't smiling like she usually was. It looks like she's afraid, Cassie thought.

Outside, Joey whispered to Cassie. "Maybe it *was* Uncle Ed that we saw at Wildwood," he said. "But why would he be sneaking around?"

Joey did a couple of wheelies on the driveway. Then he rolled back to Cassie.

"I know Granny Lee hopes he won't stay very long," Joey said in a low voice. "She told me that he never did amount to anything." He sighed. "But I know Granny Lee. She'll never turn him out."

Cassie said good-bye and walked back to her Aunt Diane's house. She noticed that tiny green apples were growing in the orchard.

When Cassie's grandfather had died, the orchard had been given to Aunt Diane. She'd hired Henry Weatherhog and Stanley Huffman to look after it for her.

Henry Weatherhog was a tall, lanky man. He always wore a big smile. But Stanley Huffman, a short and chubby man, scowled most of the time. Cassie was almost afraid of him.

Cassie gazed across the rows of apple trees. She spotted Mr. Weatherhog bouncing along on the old red tractor. He smiled when he saw her.

"Hi, Cassie!" Mr. Weatherhog called. The tractor stopped with a wheeze and a jerk. Mr. Weatherhog jumped down and walked to where Cassie stood.

"Hi, Mr. Weatherhog," said Cassie. "I see a lot of little green apples on the trees now."

"Yep," said Mr. Weatherhog. "The rain brought them out." He took off his big straw hat and wiped his brow. "You enjoying your stay here in Nebraska City?"

"Pretty much," said Cassie. "I was pretty homesick after I first got here. But I'm better now since I met Joey Ryan."

"Well, you make sure you stick around here till late August or early September," said Mr. Weatherhog. "Then you'll have a chance to bite into one of these here apples. By then they'll be big and juicy and mighty good eating."

Cassie smiled. "I'd like that," she said. "Well, so long, Mr. Weatherhog." And she continued on her way home.

As Cassie walked, she thought about Mr. Weatherhog. He's tall and thin like the man we saw at Wildwood. And like the shape I saw last night. But why would he be sneaking around like that, Cassie wondered. Then she smiled as she thought what a funny name Weatherhog was.

When Cassie got home, Aunt Diane was at the door. "Hurry, Cassie!" she said. "Your mother is on the phone."

Cassie burst into the house and ran to the phone. "Hi, Mom!" she said excitedly. "How are you?"

"I'm okay," said her mother. "How are you getting along at Aunt Diane's?"

It was so wonderful to hear her mother's voice! Cassie missed her so much she was nearly in tears. But she was determined not to cry. So she swallowed the lump that was in her throat.

"It's fine here, Mom," Cassie said. "I've made a new friend. He's in a wheelchair. We're working to earn money so he can go to a doctor in Omaha. He might be able to walk again."

"Well, honey, I think that is a very nice thing to do," Cassie's mom said. "But are you having any fun?"

"Oh sure, Mom," Cassie said. "We have lots of fun!"

"Cassie, honey," her mother said. "You mustn't worry over the divorce. Your dad and I have worked things out. You'll be with both of us a lot. And you know how much we both love you."

"All right, Mom," Cassie said.

They talked for a while longer. Then Cassie told her mother good-bye and called Aunt Diane back to the phone.

Cassie went into her room and lay down on her bed. She thought of her mom and dad, so far away in California. Their divorce made her feel sad and lonely.

At that moment, Cassie wanted so much to go home. Tears stung her eyes. And she cried softly into her pillow.

But then she thought of Joey. He sat every day in his wheelchair, never complaining. And he could never see *either one* of his parents again. Cassie was ashamed for feeling sorry for herself.

Joey seemed happy most of the time. But Cassie knew how much he wished to get out of his chair and walk again.

Maybe it isn't going to happen, Cassie thought as she dried her eyes. But if I *can* get Joey to that doctor, I'm going to do it!

Cassie sat up and blew her nose. Then she went into the bathroom and splashed cold water on her face.

Afterward, Cassie hopped back on the bed. She plumped up her pillows, reached for her book, and began reading. But as she read, her mind wandered to the night before, when she'd seen the dark figure in the backyard.

Could it have been Uncle Ed? Maybe we'll never know, she thought with a sigh.

A warm, gentle breeze blew in through the window. The lace curtains billowed. Cassie closed her eyes. Her open book slid from her hands onto the bed. As she drifted off to sleep, she thought, surely Mr. and Mrs. Wolf will pay us.

"Not fair," Cassie mumbled. "Not fair." And then she drifted off to sleep.

8
"The Money's Gone!"

Cassie and Joey worked at Wildwood for another five days. On Friday, Cassie rang the doorbell. This time, she was determined to get the money they had earned.

Mrs. Wolf came to the door with an envelope in her hand. "Here's your money," she said. "I'm sorry we didn't have it for you last week." She looked down at her rough, red hands. "Mr. Wolf and me, we've been having some hard times lately." She smiled. "You kids are doing a good job for us."

"Thanks," said Cassie and Joey.

"Whew!" said Cassie as they started down the lane. "I sure feel better now!"

"So do I," said Joey. And they hurried back to Granny Lee's house.

Joey looked around and found a jar with a lid. "I'll keep the jar in my closet," he volunteered.

Cassie and Joey walked through the living room. Uncle Ed was sprawled out on the sofa with a newspaper spread over his face. He was snoring softly. With each breath, the newspaper puffed up and back down again. Cassie giggled.

Suddenly Joey grabbed her hand and pointed outside. They both headed out.

After they were in the backyard, Cassie said, "Does Uncle Ed ever do anything to help Granny? Seems like he's always sleeping or just sitting around."

Joey shook his head. "Nope, he's a lazy old guy. That's all there is to it. I sure wish he would leave."

❊ ❊ ❊ ❊ ❊

Every weekday, Cassie and Joey trudged up the lane to Wildwood. By the middle of July, they had saved $160.

One Saturday afternoon, Cassie and Joey counted their money one more time.

"Wow!" said Cassie. "That's a *lot* of money."

"Sure is," said Joey with a grin. "What do you say we have a picnic at Arbor Lodge Park to celebrate?"

Cassie ran home and made peanut butter and jelly sandwiches. She put a bag of potato chips into her picnic basket too. Joey brought apples and some of Granny Lee's sugar cookies. Then off they went.

"It's really pretty cool to live so near a park," said Cassie as she set the picnic basket on Joey's lap.

Cassie helped Joey on the gravel road. She pushed while Joey worked the wheels with his hands.

Cassie and Joey stopped and looked in the windows of an old log cabin where Indians once lived. The door stood open just a crack.

Cassie gave the cabin door a shove. It slowly creaked open. A musty smell filled their nostrils.

It was dark and spooky inside the cabin. Over in one corner stood an old, rusty pot. There was nothing else in the cabin. Worn, old floorboards creaked as the two children moved across the floor.

"Let's get out of here," said Cassie. "It smells bad."

"Right," said Joey.

Huge shade trees cooled the park, even on hot summer days. At the far end of the park, the gravel road ended. There, it became a red brick road leading to a white mansion with big, round pillars on the porch.

The brick road was bumpy and rough. It looked very old, as though it had been there for years and years. Tufts of grass poked up between the bricks. Again, Cassie helped Joey with his wheelchair. She puffed with the effort of pushing him up a hill toward the magnificent mansion.

"The Morton family lived here a long time ago," said Joey. "I guess they had kids just like us who played around here. Do you think one of them was named Martin?"

Cassie laughed and stopped pushing Joey. She gazed at the white mansion and the beautiful lawn surrounded by flowers of every color.

"I can't imagine living in a big house like that," said Cassie. "Can you, Joey?"

"Nope," said Joey. "I sure can't. Nobody lives here anymore. People like to go through the mansion and look at all the furniture and stuff. You know. It's for tourists."

Cassie and Joey sat in the shade of a grape arbor and ate their peanut butter sandwiches. Joey reached into the picnic basket and pulled out a shiny red apple. He took a big bite and sighed contentedly.

"Cassie," Joey said. "How did you ever get the name *Cassiopeia?*"

"My dad named me," said Cassie, taking the last bite of her sandwich. "He liked to study the stars. And for some reason, the name Cassiopeia appealed to him." Cassie rummaged in the picnic basket to find her apple. "Cassiopeia is a constellation in the sky. The stars are in the shape of a chair."

"Oh," Joey said. "It's a nice name, all right. But I like Cassie better."

When Cassie and Joey were through eating, they went into a red barn. There were some old stagecoaches on display.

One of the coaches was especially pretty. It had purple fringe that hung from the roof of the carriage. It had been polished so that it gleamed.

"Look," said Cassie. "We can see our faces in the doors." Then she opened the door of the carriage and plopped down on the puffy leather seat.

"Now don't I look like a fancy lady?" Cassie asked. She made a face and piled her hair on top of her head.

"Hey, Cassie," said Joey. He was glancing around to see if anyone was looking. "You're not supposed to do that."

So Cassie jumped down. Then they started down the red brick road that led away from the mansion and out of the park.

When Cassie and Joey got to the highway, a Greyhound bus screeched and groaned to a stop. It was picking up a passenger—Uncle Ed!

Uncle Ed looked toward Cassie and Joey but didn't seem to see them. He was carrying a small black suitcase. As he climbed aboard, the door wheezed shut. Then the bus moved on down the highway.

"Well, what do you think of that?" asked Joey. "I'm sure he saw us."

"Did you know he was leaving today?" asked Cassie. She and Joey hurried across the highway before a car came.

"Nope," said Joey. "Granny didn't say anything."

Later that night, Aunt Diane's phone rang.

"The money's gone, Cassie!" said Joey. He sounded close to tears. "I looked in the jar where we stashed it. There's nothing there!"

"Where could it be?" asked Cassie. But then, she suddenly knew.

"Are you thinking what I'm thinking?" asked Joey.

"Yes," said Cassie angrily. "Uncle Ed! It must have been Uncle Ed! And I think it was Uncle Ed at Wildwood! And the night of the storm!"

"I think so too," said Joey sadly.

9
Good-Bye

Joey and Cassie told Granny Lee about their money. Her kind brown eyes filled with tears.

"I hate to think it was Ed who took your money, kids," she said. "But I don't know what else to think. It's not the first time that something has come up missing after Ed has been here." Granny Lee shook her head. "This is just terrible! I just wish I had the money to give to you."

Cassie put her arm around Granny Lee's thin shoulders. "Don't worry, Granny Lee," she said. "It's not your fault."

Granny Lee sank down on a worn kitchen chair. She shook her head in disbelief and dried her eyes.

Cassie and Joey went outside to the bench under the tall oak tree.

"Well, hey, Joey," Cassie began. "I still have nearly six weeks left before I go back to California. We can keep working at Wildwood. We won't have as much money, but at least we'll have some."

Joey looked sad. "I feel awful bad about this, Cassie," he said. "We probably should've kept our money at your Aunt Diane's house."

"Don't sweat it," said Cassie. "We'll be okay."

※ ※ ※ ※ ※

The next six weeks went by too quickly for Cassie. She had mixed feelings about leaving Nebraska City and going back home.

On their last day at Wildwood, Cassie and Joey walked slowly down the road. They didn't say much to each other.

The day was hot and humid. Clouds that had looked billowy and white against the sky a short time ago now looked dark and threatening. The wind was picking up, blowing little dust balls along the road. Now and then, a small tumbleweed rolled by.

"Looks like it might rain," said Joey.

"If it looked this way in California, there probably wouldn't be a drop of rain," Cassie said. "It hardly ever rains there in the summer."

The breeze rustling through the trees felt good on their cheeks.

"I'll bet Granny Lee will have cold lemonade for us when we get home," said Joey.

Joey was right. Granny Lee did have tart, frosty lemonade and cookies waiting for them.

While she drank, Cassie thought about the day after tomorrow. She would be leaving for California. Joey watched her with a faraway look in his eyes.

"Joey," Cassie said. "Let's write a letter to that doctor. We can find out if she'll see you for what money we've saved."

Cassie rummaged through her purse. She pulled out a crumpled piece of paper.

"Here it is," Cassie said. "This is the address."

Joey shook his head. "I don't know, Cassie," he said. "We only have $240. It's probably not enough."

"Let's try," said Cassie. She found a pen while Joey got some paper. Together, they wrote the letter.

When they were through, Cassie dug money for the stamp out of her purse.

"Let's go mail it right now," Cassie said.

When they got to the post office, Cassie bought the stamp and Joey stuck it on. As they moved to the mailbox in front of the post office, Cassie crossed her fingers.

Then, with a sigh, Joey dropped the letter into the mailbox.

✳ ✳ ✳ ✳ ✳

The next two days went by too quickly. Cassie's bags were packed. She had one thing left to do before Aunt Diane drove her to the airport.

Cassie ran down the dusty road to Joey's house.

Joey was waiting outside in his wheelchair. The two friends looked at each other for a long moment without speaking. At last, Cassie broke the awkward silence.

"Let me know as soon as you find out if Dr. Yu can help you," Cassie told Joey. "You have my address and phone number."

Cassie reached into her pocket and took out a handful of tiny seashells. "Here," she said. "You can have these to add to your others."

"Cool," said Joey. Then he reached into his shirt pocket. "This is for you." He handed Cassie a shiny gold bracelet with two lavender stones in it. "It was my mom's," he said. "I want you to have it. Granny Lee said it's all right."

Cassie slid the bracelet onto her arm. "It's beautiful, Joey," she whispered. "Thanks."

Aunt Diane tooted her car horn. The two friends said good-bye. Then Cassie ran up the road and climbed into the car.

When they turned onto the road, Cassie turned and waved. Joey waved back. "Come back next summer?" he called after her.

"Maybe," Cassie answered. Tears blurred her vision. "Let me know, okay?"

Joey waved in answer.

※ ※ ※ ※ ※

Things at home were going better than Cassie had thought they would. Her parents got along better now, even though they weren't living together.

During the second week of school, Cassie returned home and saw a letter on the table. It was addressed to her! And it was from Joey!

Dear Cassie,

I hope things are going well for you in California. School has started here and we're back to the same old thing—homework! I'd rather be working for the Wolfs!

Guess what? Dr. Yu from the Clarkson Hospital in Omaha finally called! She wants to see me! She said not to worry about the money. She said we'd work something out! Isn't that great!

Your Aunt Diane is going to drive me and Granny Lee to Omaha next Wednesday. I think that is really nice of her.

I guess we'll find out more after the appointment. Granny Lee doesn't want me to get my hopes up. But I'm afraid they already are.

Will you come back next summer?
Love, Joey

Maybe, Cassie thought. And when I go back, maybe Joey will be walking.

And wouldn't it be funny if Dr. Yu's first name was Olive?